Ros Asquith

FIBBY LIBBY

A SHARK ATE MY SOCKS

Happy Cat Books
Published by Catnip Publishing Ltd.
14 Greville Street
London
EC1N 8SB

This edition published 2009
1 3 5 7 9 10 8 6 4 2

A CIP catalogue record for this book is available from the British Library

ISBN 978-1-905117-62-8

CHAPTER ONE

Ever had the feeling you'd like to be someone else?

Libby did.

Every day and in every way, Libby wanted to be different.

Not that there was anything wrong with Libby. She was quite normal.

Head → Important bit on top of body (with a face on front)

← Twig-coloured hair

← Smudgy skin

Normal cardy with buttons and 2 sleeves for posting arms through

Body → Squarish bit joining head to legs

Hand placed on end of arm to stop fraying

2 Knees (only bend one way, so sticking plaster goes on front bit)

Pair of feet → At end of legs to balance and propel

← **Sensible Sandals** "Allow feet to breathe" (what does this MEAN?)

Normal muddish-coloured eyes, twig-coloured hair, smudge-coloured skin and so forth. (Libby never did understand why anyone was called 'black' or 'white' – made them sound like a bunch of penguins..!).

Roof (at top)

Window (glass, so you can see out)

Door (at bottom, so you can go in and out without learning to fly).

Libby lived in a normal house …

… in a normal street …

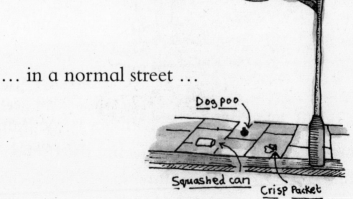

Dog poo

Squashed can

Crisp Packet

and, because it was normal, she was even quite friendly, in a mild sort of way, with Karen, the very normal girl who lived next door.

Karen-next-door

But Karen-next-door, with her beige hair, fawn socks and sandals, was not the friend that Libby dreamed of having.

Libby dreamed of an exciting girl, a long-lost twin sister perhaps, with jet black hair. Libby wished and wished for a sister.

Or a horse. But normal families like Libby's don't have horses in their back yards.

"Though it would make lovely manure for the window boxes," said Libby's distressingly normal mum.

Libby's parents were not the kind of parents who stood out in a crowd.

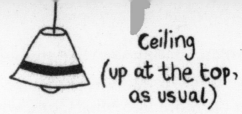

Sometimes, guiltily, Libby would dream of having different parents.

Ones a bit more like Aunt Cora, who had brought her a scarlet dress from Spain.

Libby loved that dress, but she only put it on in her bedroom.

In the evenings, while eating her ham, boiled potatoes and peas, Libby would dream of Bombe Suprise, which, as far as she knew, was an exotic dish from a far-off land. (In fact, it was ice-cream and glâcé cherries, available from Shop-a-Lot down the road.)

Spanish dresses, exotic food and far-off lands were dreams Libby usually kept to herself.

But she wanted so much to be different, that she decided to do something Very Unusual Indeed . . .

CHAPTER TWO

The next day, when Miss Wilderness, the very normal teacher at Libby's disappointingly normal school, asked her to tell the class what she had done in the holidays, Libby suddenly became shy.

"I can't," she blushed, "my mum told me not to boast."

This had the desired effect.

"Go on," said Barbara, who could do backwards somersaults and had never spoken to Libby before.

"Tell!" said Yasmin, who could wiggle her ears, and often wiggled them at the admiring Libby.

"What happened?" shouted Billy King, who could do his times tables without a calculator, and had never so much as looked at Libby in his life.

Karen-next-door went very quiet and gazed at her sandals.
Even Miss Wilderness, whose eyes had never been seen to stretch, nor her brow to shift, murmured soft encouragement.
Libby held out a little longer, until the swell of interest had grown, if not to fever pitch, at least to a higher level than normal. Then, with just the right degree of modesty, and no small amount of blushing, she spoke:

"We were at the beach. It was an amazing, exotic FLORIDA beach with palm trees. It was blazing hot. My mum was just taking out her watercolours to do one of her brilliant paintings which sell for a fortune in London galleries. My dad was settling down with a very difficult crossword, when suddenly there was a terrible, ear-splitting, nerve-wracking, shrill, scary SCREAM!"

THE TRUTH

Libby's parents could not afford a beach holiday as her father had just lost his job.

It had been a wonderful job making holes in doughnuts, but Libby had always eaten everything except the bit he made, which made him sad, but not as sad as losing his job had made him.

So, one blazing hot morning, they decided to spend a day at the fabulous Lido Leisure Complex.

They had just settled down when there was a loud SCREAM . . .

Ah well, at least we could afford one day at the Leisure Complex

Welcome to the FLORiD Pleasure Dome!
Mmm... Lovely - apart from the NOISE
changing rooms
water chutes
HOW TO DO IT
Making holes in mints....
ARRGHH!

"Guess what had happened!
A poor little girl was waving her arms about in the plunging foam. She had fallen off her li-lo and was about to be swept up in a huge, vast, GYNORMOUS, hurricane of a wave!!"

"**And in that wave was something pointed . . . and black . . . and menacing . . . it was . . . it was . . .**"

Libby couldn't say any more. With true performer's timing, she allowed her audience to gasp out the magic words for her . . .

A SHARK'S FIN!

THE TRUTH

Just as the Lido Leisure Complex had started its wave machine, a poor little girl was seen waving her arms about in the foam.

She was about to be covered by a ripple at least the height of a mouse, or possibly that of a moderately-sized bat.

And in that ripple was
something pointed,
and black,
and menacing.

It was . . .

it was . . .

A shark's fin!

"I was horrified! My dad can't swim on account of his war-wound. My mum can't swim on account of her tragic disease. There was no-one else on the beach. It was deserted. It was a wilderness, Miss Wilderness, a wilderness! I was the only one who could possibly save the poor little mite from a terrible fate."

But you can only swim one **WIDTH** of the **BABY POOL!**

Yeah! And that's with **armbands!**

"So, I grabbed my armbands and my li-lo, and a length of chain which was lying nearby, and I ran, swifter than a speeding bullet, faster than the speed of light, as quick as . . . as a volcano . . . down the beach towards the plunging foam . . ."

CHAPTER THREE

THE TRUTH

Libby's father couldn't swim because he had sprained his arm while washing an egg-cup. Libby's mother couldn't swim because she'd never had a swimming lesson in her life (although she could float in shallow water, as long as she thought only of rice pudding and hot water bottles).

As a result, Libby's parents insisted that Libby wore armbands and a life jacket whenever she was near anything wet – even a puddle.

So, when they heard wild screams of

"SHARK!" and

"HELP, SHARK!" and

"AARGGGHHH!!!"

… they didn't think for a moment that the cries might be coming from their only child, Libby herself!

" 'Don't worry about me, Mum,' I shouted, as I raced helter-skelter down to the tidal waves crashing wildly on the coral reef.

'No, No! Libby! Don't go! You'll drown!' she cried, but her words were lost in the raging whirlwind that had blown up out of the wild . . . ummm . . . plains."

"I flung my li-lo into the surf—"

Libby raced on, sure that if she spoke fast enough, she could erase the look of disbelief that had just crossed Miss Wilderness's face.

"—and paddled furiously towards the sharp, black, menacing . . ."

"And there, in the swirling, raging, sparkling, furious foam, I saw a pale, limp, soaking little hand and grabbed it! And I pulled with all the force of a thousand army tanks until the frail mite was beside me on the li-lo, with scarlet, red, crimson gore, dripping from the gash on her leg where she had been bitten by the . . . the . . ."

"So, I swung my chain around my head and flung it at the shark--"

(At this point, Libby demonstrated with her belt.)

THE TRUTH

It was only when somebody tapped Libby's mother on the shoulder and asked her if it was *her* child who seemed to have injured herself, that Libby's mother looked up:

Libby rushed on:

"... Finally, after what seemed like many hours on the roaring ocean ..."

CHAPTER FOUR

"The next day my picture was in the papers alongside the handsome golden man. The headline was 'HEROIC RESCUE' *and* he paid for my father's operation.

So, now you can see why my mum told me not to boast."

Libby stood gazing at her classmates through lowered lashes, and twiddled a strand of twig-coloured hair between her fluttering fingers.

THE TRUTH

The lifeguard, hearing the call for help walked into the ripple as far as his ankles. He removed Libby from the path of the plastic inflatable shark which was frightening her. Then he soothed the teeny scratch she had got from its fin with a sticking plaster covered in pictures of hedgehogs in party dresses.

The photographer at the Lido Leisure Complex was charmed by the sight of Libby and the handsome, golden-haired lifeguard. Sure enough, a picture of them standing side by side appeared on the front of the Lido newsletter.

Libby's dad was pleased because the lifeguard gave him some excellent advice on sprains. Libby was pleased as she was able to cut out the picture from the Lido newsletter, and stick it on the wall by her bed.

CHAPTER FIVE

Naturally, once Libby had finished telling her story, everyone crowded round and told her she was the bravest, most exciting person in the world.

A long queue of children wanting her autograph formed in the playground.

Billy said what was the use of times tables?

Barbara said she didn't think Libby
had it in her, and this just proved that
somersaulting backwards wasn't the only
thing worth doing.

Yasmin confessed that there was more to life than ear-wiggling.

Only Karen-next-door was quiet. She's jealous, thought Libby, because she's normal and I'm not.

More and more children crowded around Libby as the story spread throughout the school. Someone said that the Headteacher, Mrs Ironhand, was going to give Libby a medal!

This was great. This was just what Libby wanted. She wasn't normal anymore, she was very, very different. Nobody in this normal school, in this extremely normal street, in this very normal town, had ever rescued anyone from a SHARK before. No way.

SO WHY WAS LIBBY FEELING SO UNWELL?

Because Libby knew that her story had been, well, not *exactly* true . . .

And she couldn't help having the sneaky feeling that Karen-next-door, might just know that the Normals hadn't been to Florida at all.

And Libby knew that when her mum came to pick her up at home time, that some of the children might, um, well, ask her mother about it, and . . .

Libby felt very unwell indeed.

Libby went to the office and asked to go home early. The school secretary rang Libby's mum.

Libby's mum was out. So was her dad. So was her Aunt Cora, who sometimes picked her up.

Libby had to wait.

Libby felt sick.

Libby felt very sick.

Libby was very sick. All over the office carpet.

But **YOU DON'T** want to see **THAT,** do you?

"I think I better go to hospital," she gasped, seeing a ray of sunshine and a hope of escape.

"No, dear," said the school secretary kindly, "It's nearly home time. Mum'll be here soon."

A wave of panic surged through Libby, who felt as if her head was going to explode, or roll off. In fact, she wished it would.

Libby was just debating whether to run for it, or jump through the office window, (it was only on the first floor) when the bell rang.

Too late. No escape. She would be found out. She would be laughed at forever . . . she would never be normal again. Oh, how she *wished* she had told the . . .

CHAPTER SIX

Sure enough, as she gazed like a prisoner through the murky office window, she saw her mother, submerged in a sea of children. Their voices floated up to her. And this is what she heard:

Was'er photo REALLY in the paper?

Fancy Libby in all them WAVES!

AMAZING about the SHARK!

What a FANTASTIC RESCUE

YEAH! An' all the BLOOD!

And then, to Libby's horror, she saw the form of Miss Wilderness approaching. What would she say?

We **DID** enjoy Libby's story of the **SHARK. SO** brave... and I'm **SO** pleased that your husband's arm is better

Libby thought she was going to faint. Then, through the gabble of voices, she heard her mother's reply:

Mmmm.... the waves **WERE** rather high.... Mmmm the **SHARK WAS** amazing..... Oh, there wasn't **that** much **BLOOD**... ah, YES, **LOVELY** photo... YES, she was very brave....

Suddenly, Libby's mother didn't seem normal any more. She was a heroine, a tigress defending her young. She swept through the admiring crowd, and collected her dazed daughter from the sick room.

Sword of JUSTICE

Shield of COURAGE

CHAPTER SEVEN

Libby went to bed immediately she got home and lay there, exhausted.

She had been going to thank her mother when she realised the truth.

The waves at the Lido Leisure Complex *had* been large. The inflatable shark *was* **amazingly** lifelike. And, as far as Libby's mum was concerned, she *had* been really brave. Because, to Libby's mum, going anywhere near the water was an act of courage worthy of a medal.

Libby's mother came to see how she was feeling.

"I've bought you some of Mr Bellyache's home-baked apple pie and custard. Sorry about the lumps."

"Oh, and a get-well-soon card from Karen-next-door. Isn't that sweet of her?"

To heroic
Libby
(HO ho ho)

It was a full twenty minutes before Libby
could bring herself to open the envelope,
by which time she had decided she would
have to leave the country. Despairingly,
tremblingly, she pulled out the card.

Inside, it read:

Get Well Soon

Don't worry
I won't tell.
Love, K.

There was more to Karen-next-door
than Libby had thought, after all.

Look out for more adventures starring
Fibby Libby

Ros Asquith
FIBBY LIBBY
A GHOST ATE MY TOAST
Libby - the little girl with the HUGE imagination!